My Favourite
Fairy
Tales

Produced for Chad Valley Toys
242–246 Marylebone Road
London, NW1 6JL
www.woolworths.co.uk

Writers: Aneurin Rhys and Ronne Randall
Illustrators: Chameleon Design

ISBN 1-40545-998-0

Printed in China

My Favourite
Fairy Tales

p

CONTENTS

CONTENTS

The Three
Little Pigs

Once upon a time, there were three little pigs who lived with their mummy in a big stone house.

One day, Mummy Pig said, "Children, it's time for you to go out and find your fortune in the big wide world." So she packed a little bag of food and a drink for each of them, and sent them on their way.

"Goodbye!" she called, as the three little pigs set off on their adventure. "Good luck, my dears, and remember to watch out for the big, bad wolf!"

"We will, Mummy," called the little pigs as they waved goodbye.

After a while, the three little pigs stopped for a rest and decided that they should each build a house to live in. Just then, they saw a farmer coming along the road with a wagon full of golden straw.

"Please, sir," said the first little pig, "may I have some of your straw to build myself a house?"

"Yes, little pig," said the farmer, "of course you can."

So the first little pig built his house of straw. Soon it was finished. It looked very good indeed, and the first little pig was happy.

The other two little pigs set off on their journey together and, after a while, they met a man carrying a large bundle of sticks.

"Please, sir," said the second little pig, "may I have some of your sticks to build myself a house?"

"Yes, little pig," said the man, "of course you can."

So the second little pig built his house of sticks. Soon it was finished. It looked very good indeed, and the second little pig was happy.

The third little pig set off on his journey alone. He saw lots of people with wagons of straw and bundles of sticks, but he did not stop until he met a man with a cart filled to the brim with bricks.

"Please, sir," said the third little pig, "may I have some bricks to build myself a house?"

"Yes, little pig," said the man, "of course you can."

So the third little pig built his house of bricks. Soon it was finished. It looked very good indeed. It was strong and solid, and the third little pig was very, very pleased.

That evening, the big, bad wolf was walking along the road. He was very hungry and looking for something good to eat. He saw the first little pig's house of straw and looked in through the window.

"Yum, yum," he said to himself, licking his lips. "This little pig would make a most tasty dinner."

So in his friendliest voice, the wolf called through the window, "Little pig, little pig, please let me in!"

But the first little pig remembered his Mummy's warning, so he replied, "No, no, I won't let you in, not by the hair on my chinny-chin-chin!"

This made the wolf really angry. "Very well!" he roared. "I'll huff and I'll puff, and I'll blow your house down!"

The poor little pig was very afraid, but he still would not let the wolf in. So the wolf huffed... and he puffed... and he BLEW the straw house down.

Then the big, bad wolf chased the little pig and - gobbled him up!

But the wolf was still hungry! He walked down the road and soon came to the house made of sticks. He looked through the window and called to the second little pig, "Little pig, little pig, please let me in."

"No, no!" cried the second little pig. "I won't let you in, not by the hair on my chinny-chin-chin!"

"Very well," cried the wolf. "Then I'll huff and I'll puff, and I'll blow your house down!"

And that's just what the big, bad wolf did. He huffed... and he puffed... and he BLEW the stick house down! Then he gobbled up the second little pig.

But the big, bad wolf was still hungry.
So he walked down the road and soon
came to the house made of bricks. He
looked through the window and
called to the third little pig, "Little
pig, little pig, please let me in."

"No, no!" cried the third little pig.
"I won't let you in, not by the hair
on my chinny-chin-chin!"

"Very well," roared the big, bad
wolf. "I'll huff and I'll puff, and I'll
blow your house down!"

So the wolf huffed and he puffed...
he HUFFED and he PUFFED... and
he HUFFED and he PUFFED some
more, but he could not blow the
brick house down!

By now the big, bad wolf was very, very angry. He scrambled up onto the roof and began to climb down through the chimney.

But the third little pig was a clever little pig, and he had put a big pot of boiling water to bubble on the fire.

When the wolf came down the chimney, he landed - ker-splosh! - right in the middle of the pot of boiling water! He burned his bottom so badly that he ran out of the house and down the road as fast as his legs could carry him, and was never heard of again!

The third little pig was very pleased
with his house of bricks and lived in
it for many years, happy and content.
And nothing was heard of the big,
bad wolf ever again.

Puss in Boots

There was once a miller who had three sons. When he died, he left his mill to the eldest son, his cottage to his middle son and only his pet cat to his youngest son, William.

William went and sat under a tree, feeling very miserable and sorry for himself. "What will become of us, Puss?" he moaned.

To William's utter amazement, Puss answered him. "Don't worry, Master," said the cat. "Just do what I say and you will be far richer than either of your brothers!"

Puss told William to get him a fine
suit of clothes, a pair of soft leather
boots and a strong canvas sack. Then
he caught a huge rabbit, put it in the
sack, and took it to the palace.

No one there had ever seen a talking
cat before, so he was granted an
immediate audience with the king.

"Your Majesty," said Puss, "this fine
rabbit is a gift from my master, the
Marquis of Carabas."

The king had never heard of the
Marquis of Carabas, but he was too
embarrassed to admit this. "Please
thank the Marquis," he said to Puss,
"and give him my regards."

The next day, Puss caught some plump partridges and once more he took them to the king, with the same message: "These are from my master."

For several months, Puss went on bringing the king fine gifts.

One day, he heard that the king would be riding along the river bank that afternoon with the princess.

"Master," said Puss, "you must go swimming in the river today."

"Why?" asked William.

"Just do as I say, and you will see," answered Puss.

While William was swimming, Puss hid all his clothes. Then, when he saw the king's carriage approaching, he ran up to it shouting for help. "Help!" cried Puss. "Robbers have stolen my master's clothes!"

When the king recognised the cat, he immediately called to his chief steward and ordered him to bring a fine new suit from the palace.

"It must be of the finest cut," said the king, "and made from the softest cloth, do you hear! Only the best will do for the Marquis of Carabas!"

Once he was dressed in his fine new suit, William looked quite handsome. The princess invited him to join her and her father in the carriage.

As William and the princess sat side by side, they began to fall in love.

Meanwhile, Puss ran ahead until he came to a meadow where he saw some men mowing. "The king's carriage is coming," Puss told them. "When he asks whose meadow this is, say it belongs to the Marquis of Carabas - or you will have your heads cut off!"

The mowers didn't dare to disobey.

When the royal carriage came by, the king asked who the meadow belonged to. The mowers quickly replied, "The Marquis of Carabas."

"I can see that you are very well off indeed," the king said to William, who blushed modestly. That made the princess love him even more!

Down the road, Puss came to a field where men were harvesting corn.

"When the king asks whose corn this is," Puss told them, "say it belongs to the Marquis of Carabas – or you will have your heads cut off!"

The harvesters didn't dare to disobey.

Next, Puss came to an enormous castle which he knew belonged to a fierce ogre. Still he bravely knocked on the door.

When the ogre let him in, Puss bowed low and said, "I have heard that you have wondrous powers, and can change yourself into anything - even a lion or an elephant."

"That is true," said the ogre. And to prove it, he changed himself into a snarling, growling lion.

Puss was terrified and leapt up onto a cupboard. Then the ogre changed himself back again.

"That was amazing," Puss remarked. "But surely it cannot be too difficult for someone of your size to change into a creature as big as a lion. If you were truly the magician they say you are, you could turn into something tiny - like a mouse."

"Of course I can do that!" bellowed the ogre. In an instant he became a little brown mouse scurrying across the floor.

Quick as a flash, Puss leapt off the cupboard, pounced on the mouse and ate it in one big gulp!

Soon, Puss heard the king's carriage drawing near and rushed outside. As it approached, he bowed low and said, "Welcome, Your Majesty, to the home of the Marquis of Carabas."

The king was very impressed indeed. "May we come in?" he asked William.

"Of course, Your Majesty," replied William, a little confused.

As they walked through the castle, the King was delighted to see treasures of great value everywhere he looked. He was so pleased that he said to William, "You are the perfect husband for my daughter."

William and the princess were very happy and later that day they were married. They lived in the ogre's castle happily ever after. Puss, of course, lived with them – though he never chased mice again!

Goldilocks and the Three Bears

Once upon a time, there lived a family of bears: great big Daddy Bear, middle-sized Mummy Bear and little Baby Bear.

One sunny morning, Daddy Bear cooked three bowls of porridge for breakfast. When he poured it into the bowls, it was far too hot to eat!

"Let's go for a walk while our porridge cools down," said Mummy Bear.

The three bears left the bowls of porridge on the table and went for a walk.

The sun was shining brightly through the trees that morning and someone else was walking in the forest. It was a little girl called Goldilocks, who had long, curly golden hair and the cutest nose you ever did see.

Goldilocks was skipping happily through the forest when suddenly she smelt something yummy and delicious - whatever could it be?

She followed the smell until she came to the three bears' cottage. It seemed to be coming from inside. The door was open, so she peeped in and saw three bowls of porridge on the table.

Goldilocks just couldn't resist the lovely sweet smell. So, even though she knew she wasn't ever supposed to go into anyone's house without first being invited, she tiptoed inside.

First, she tasted the porridge in Daddy Bear's great big bowl. "Ouch!" she said. "This porridge is *far* too hot!" So she tried the porridge in Mummy Bear's middle-sized bowl. "Yuck!" said Goldilocks. "This porridge is *far* too sweet!" Finally, she tried the porridge in Baby Bear's tiny little bowl. "Yummy!" she said, licking her lips. "This porridge is *just right*!" So Goldilocks ate it *all* up - every last drop!

Goldilocks was so full up after eating Baby Bear's porridge that she decided she must sit down. First, she tried sitting in Daddy Bear's great big chair. "Oh, dear!" she said. "This chair is *far* too hard!" So she tried Mummy Bear's middle-sized chair. "Oh, no!" said Goldilocks. "This chair is *far* too soft!" Finally, Goldilocks tried Baby Bear's tiny little chair. "Hurray!" she cried. "This chair is *just right*!" So she stretched out and made herself very comfortable.

But Baby Bear's chair wasn't *just right*! It was *far* too small and, as Goldilocks settled down, it broke into lots of little pieces!

Goldilocks picked herself up off the floor and brushed down her dress. Trying out all of those chairs had made her *very* tired. She looked around the cottage for a place to lie down and soon found the three bears' bedroom.

First, Goldilocks tried Daddy Bear's great big bed. "Oh, this won't do!" she said. "This bed is *far* too hard!" So she tried Mummy Bear's middle-sized bed. "Oh, bother!" said Goldilocks. "This bed is *far* too soft!" Finally, she tried Baby Bear's tiny little bed. "Yippee!" she cried. "This bed is *just right*!" So Goldilocks climbed in, pulled the blanket up to her chin and fell fast, fast asleep.

Not long after, the three bears came home from their walk, ready for their yummy porridge. But as soon as they entered their little cottage, they knew something wasn't quite right.

"Someone's been eating my porridge!" said Daddy Bear, when he looked at his great big bowl.

"Someone's been eating my porridge!" said Mummy Bear, looking at her middle-sized bowl.

"Someone's been eating *my* porridge," cried Baby Bear, looking sadly at his tiny little bowl. "And they've eaten it *all up*!"

Then Daddy Bear noticed that his chair had been moved. "Look, Mummy Bear! Someone's been sitting in my chair!" he said in his deep, gruff voice.

"Look, Daddy Bear! Someone's been sitting in my chair," said Mummy Bear, as she straightened the cushions on it.

"Someone's been sitting in *my* chair, too," cried Baby Bear. "And look! They've broken it all to pieces!" They all stared at the bits of broken chair. Then Baby Bear burst into tears.

Suddenly, the three bears heard the tiniest of noises. Was it a creak? Was it a groan? No, it was a snore, and it was coming from their bedroom. They crept up the stairs very, very quietly, to see what was making the noise...

"Someone's been sleeping in my bed!" cried Daddy Bear.

"Someone's been sleeping in my bed," said Mummy Bear.

"Someone's been sleeping in *my* bed!" cried Baby Bear. "And she's still there!"

All this noise woke Goldilocks up with a start.

When she saw the three bears
standing over her, Goldilocks was
very scared. "Oh, dear! Oh, dear!
Oh, dear!" she cried, jumping out of
Baby Bear's bed. She ran out of the
bedroom, down the stairs, out of the
front door and all the way back
home – and she never ever came back
to the forest again!

Cinderella

Once upon a time, there lived a pretty little girl. When she was young, her mother sadly died. Her father remarried, but the girl's stepmother was a mean woman with two ugly daughters. These stepsisters were so jealous of the young girl's beauty that they treated her like a servant and made her sit among the cinders in the kitchen.

They called her Cinderella, and before long everyone, even her father, had forgotten the little girl's real name. Cinderella missed her real mother more and more each day.

One day, an invitation arrived from the royal palace. The king and queen were holding a ball for the prince's twenty-first birthday, and all the fine ladies of the kingdom were invited.

Cinderella's stepsisters were very excited when their invitations arrived.

"I will wear my red velvet gown!" cried the first stepsister. "And the black pearl necklace that Mother gave to me."

"And I will wear my blue silk dress!" cried the other. "With a silver tiara."

"Come, Cinderella!" they called. "You must help us to get ready!"

Cinderella helped her stepsisters with their silk stockings and frilly petticoats. She brushed and curled their hair and powdered their cheeks and noses. At last, she squeezed them into their beautiful ball-gowns.

But even after all this, the two ugly stepsisters weren't nearly as lovely as Cinderella was in her rags. This made them very jealous and angry, and they began to tease Cinderella.

"Too bad you can't come to the ball, Cinders!" sneered the first stepsister.

"Yes," laughed the other one. "They'd never let a shabby creature like you near the palace!"

Cinderella said nothing, but inside, her heart was breaking. She really wanted to go to the ball. After her stepsisters left, she sat and wept.

"Dry your tears, my dear," said a gentle voice.

Cinderella was amazed. A kind old woman stood before her. In her hand was a sparkly wand that shone.

"I am your Fairy Godmother," she told Cinderella. "And you shall go to the ball!"

"But I have nothing to wear! And how will I get there?" cried Cinderella.

The Fairy Godmother smiled!

The Fairy Godmother asked Cinders to fetch her the biggest pumpkin in the garden. With a flick of her magic wand she turned it into a golden carriage and the mice in the kitchen mousetrap into fine horses. A fat rat soon became a handsome coachman.

Cinderella couldn't believe her eyes.

Smiling, the Fairy Godmother waved her wand once more and suddenly Cinderella was dressed in a splendid ball-gown. On her feet were sparkling glass slippers.

"My magic will end at midnight, so you must be home before then," said the Fairy Godmother. "Good luck."

When Cinderella arrived at the ball, everyone was dazzled by her beauty. Whispers went round the ballroom as the other guests wondered who this enchanting stranger could be. Even Cinderella's own stepsisters did not recognise her.

As soon as the prince set eyes on Cinderella, he fell in love with her. "Would you do me the honour of this dance?" he asked.

"Why certainly, sir," Cinderella answered. And from that moment on he only had eyes for Cinderella.

Soon the clock struck midnight. "I must go!" said Cinderella, suddenly remembering her promise to her Fairy Godmother. She fled from the ballroom and ran down the palace steps. The prince ran after her, but when he got outside, she was gone. He didn't notice a grubby servant girl holding a pumpkin. A few mice and a rat scurried around her feet.

But there on the steps was one dainty glass slipper. The prince picked it up and rushed back into the palace. "Does anyone know who this slipper belongs to?" he cried.

The next day, Cinderella's stepsisters could talk of nothing but the ball, and the beautiful stranger who had danced all night with the prince. As they were talking, there was a knock at the door.

"Cinderella," called the stepmother, "quick, jump to it and see who it is." Standing on the doorstep was His Highness the Prince and a royal footman, who was holding the little glass slipper on a velvet cushion.

"The lady whose foot this slipper fits is my one and only true love," said the prince. "I am visiting every house in the kingdom in search of her."

The two stepsisters began shoving each other out of the way in their rush to try on the slipper. They both squeezed and pushed as hard as they could, but their clumsy feet were far too big for the tiny glass shoe.

Then Cinderella stepped forward. "Please, Your Highness," she said, shyly, "may I try?"

As her stepsisters watched in utter amazement, Cinderella slid her foot into the dainty slipper. It fitted as if it were made for her!

As the prince gazed into her eyes, he knew he had found his love - and Cinderella knew she had found hers.

Cinderella and the prince soon set a date to be married.

On the day of their wedding, the land rang to the sound of bells, and the sun shone as the people cheered. Even Cinderella's nasty stepsisters were invited. Everyone had a really wonderful day, and Cinderella and her prince lived happily ever after.

Snow White

Long, long ago, in a faraway land, there lived a king and queen who had a beautiful baby girl. Her lips were as red as cherries, her hair as black as coal and her skin as white as snow - her name was Snow White.

Sadly, the queen died and years later the king married again. The new queen was very beautiful, but also evil, cruel and vain. She had a magic mirror, and every day she looked into it and asked, "Mirror, mirror on the wall, who is the fairest one of all?"

And every day, the mirror replied, "You, O Queen, are the fairest!"

Time passed, and every year Snow White grew more beautiful by the hour. The queen became increasingly jealous of her stepdaughter.

One day, the magic mirror gave the queen a different answer to her question. "Snow White is the fairest one of all!" it replied.

The queen was furious. She ordered her huntsman to take Snow White deep into the forest and kill her.

But the huntsman couldn't bear to harm Snow White. "Run away!" he told her. "Run away and never come back, or the queen will kill us both!" Snow White fled deep into the forest.

As Snow White rushed through the trees she came upon a tiny cottage. She knocked at the door and then went in - the house was empty. There she found a tiny table with seven tiny chairs. Upstairs there were seven little beds. Exhausted, she lay down across them and fell asleep.

Many hours later, Snow White woke to see seven little faces peering at her. The dwarfs, who worked in a diamond mine, had returned home and wanted to know who the pretty young girl was.

Snow White told them her story and why she had to run away. They all sat round and listened to her tale.

When she had finished, the eldest dwarf said, "If you will look after our house for us, we will keep you safe. But please don't let anyone into the cottage while we are at work!"

The next morning, when the wicked queen asked the mirror her usual question, she was horrified when it answered, "The fairest is Snow White, gentle and good. She lives in a cottage, deep in the wood!"

The queen turned green with rage; she had been tricked. She magically disguised herself as an old pedlar and set off into the wood to seek out Snow White and kill the girl herself.

That afternoon, Snow White heard a tap-tapping at the window. She looked out and saw an old woman with a basket full of bright ribbons and laces.

"Pretty things for sale," cackled the old woman.

Snow White remembered the dwarfs' warning. But the ribbons and laces were so lovely, and the woman seemed so harmless, that she let her in.

"Try this new lace in your dress, my dear," said the old woman. Snow White was thrilled and let the lady thread the laces. But they were pulled so tight that Snow White fainted.

Certain that at last she had killed her stepdaughter, the queen raced through the forest, back to her castle, laughing evilly.

That evening, the dwarfs returned home. They were shocked to discover Snow White lying on the floor - lifeless. They loosened the laces on her dress so she could breathe and made her promise once again not to let any strangers in when they were at work.

The next day, when the mirror told the queen that Snow White was still alive, she was livid and vowed to kill her once and for all. She disguised herself and went back to the cottage.

This time the old woman took with her a basket of lovely red apples. She had poisoned the biggest, reddest one of all. She knocked on the door and called out, "Juicy red apples for sale."

The apples looked so delicious that Snow White just had to buy one. She opened the door and let the old woman in. "My, what pretty, rosy cheeks you have, deary," said the woman, "the very colour of my apples. Here, take a bite and see how good they are." She handed Snow White the biggest one...

Snow White took a large bite and fell to the floor - dead. The old woman fled into the forest, happy at last.

This time, the dwarfs could not bring Snow White back to life. Overcome with grief, they placed her gently in a glass coffin and carried it to a quiet clearing in the forest. And there they sat, keeping watch over their beloved Snow White.

One day, a handsome young prince came riding through the forest and saw the beautiful young girl in the glass coffin. He fell in love with her at once and begged the dwarfs to let him take her back to his castle.

At first the dwarfs refused, but when they saw how much the prince loved their Snow White, they agreed.

As the prince lifted the coffin to carry it away, he stumbled, and the piece of poisoned apple fell from Snow White's mouth, where it had been lodged all this time. Snow White's eyes fluttered open, and she looked up and saw the handsome young man.

"Where am I?" she asked him in a bewildered voice. "Who are you?"

"I am your prince," he said. "And you are safe with me now. Please will you marry me and come to live in my castle!" He leant forward and kissed her cheek.

"Oh, yes sweet prince," cried Snow White. "Of course I will."

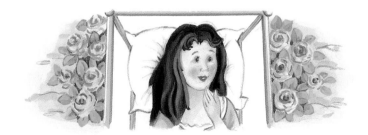

The next day, the magic mirror told the wicked queen of Snow White's good fortune. She flew into a rage and disappeared in a flash of lightning.

Snow White married her prince, and went to live in his castle. The seven dwarfs visited them often, and Snow White and her prince lived happily ever after.

Little Red Riding Hood

Once upon a time there was a little girl who lived with her mother at the edge of a deep, dark forest. Everyone called the girl 'Little Red Riding Hood', because she always wore a bright red cloak with a bright red hood.

One sunny morning her mother said, "Granny isn't feeling very well. Please will you take this basket of goodies to her, to make her feel better?"

"I will," replied Little Red Riding Hood.

"Remember," said her mother, "stay on the path, and don't stop to talk to any strangers on the way."

Little Red Riding Hood hopped and skipped along the path to Granny's house. She had only gone a short way into the deep, dark forest, when a sly, nasty wolf with big shiny teeth and long sharp claws jumped out onto the path, right in front of her.

"Hello, my pretty one," said the wolf. "Where are you going on this fine morning?"

"Good morning," said Little Red Riding Hood politely. "I'm going to see my granny, who isn't feeling very well. She lives all the way on the other side of the forest. But please excuse me, I am not allowed to talk to strangers."

"Of course little girl," sneered the crafty wolf. "You must be in a hurry. Why not take a moment to pick a big bunch of these lovely wildflowers to cheer your granny up?"

"Thank you Mr Wolf, that sounds like a very good idea," said Little Red Riding Hood, putting her basket down on the ground. "I'm sure that Granny would love them."

So, while Little Red Riding Hood picked a bunch of sweet-smelling flowers, the wicked wolf raced ahead through the deep, dark forest and soon arrived at Granny's pretty cottage.

The wolf lifted the knocker and banged hard at the door.

Sweet old Granny sat up in bed. "Who is it?" she called.

"It's me, Little Red Riding Hood," replied the wolf in a voice just like Little Red Riding Hood's.

"Hello, my dear," called Granny. "The door is not locked - lift up the latch and come in."

So the wolf opened the door and, quick as a flash, he gobbled Granny up. Then he put on her nightie and nightcap, and crawled under the bedcovers to lie in wait for Little Red Riding Hood.

A short time later, Little Red Riding Hood arrived at the cottage and knocked on Granny's door.

"Who is it?" called the wolf, in a voice just like Granny's.

"It's me, Granny," came the reply, "Little Red Riding Hood."

"Hello, my dear," called the wolf. "The door is not locked - lift up the latch and come in."

So Little Red Riding Hood lifted the latch, opened the door and went into Granny's cottage.

Little Red Riding Hood couldn't believe her eyes. "Oh, Granny," she said, "it is so nice to see you, but what big ears you have!"

"All the better to hear you with," said the wolf. "Come closer, my dear."

Little Red Riding Hood took a step closer to the bed.

"Oh, Granny," she said, "what big eyes you have!"

"All the better to see you with," said the wolf. "Come closer, my dear."

So Little Red Riding Hood took another step closer. Now she was right beside Granny's bed.

"Oh, Granny!" she cried. "What big teeth you have!

"All the better to eat you with, my dear!" snarled the wolf, and he jumped up and swallowed Little Red Riding Hood in one BIG gulp!

Now it just so happened that a woodcutter was passing Granny's cottage that sunny morning. He was going to work on the other side of the forest. He knew that Granny had not been feeling very well, so he decided to look in on her.

What a surprise he had when he saw the hairy wolf fast asleep in Granny's bed!

When he saw the wolf's big, fat tummy, he knew just what had happened.

Quick as a flash, he took out his shiny sharp axe and sliced the wolf open! Out popped Granny and Little Red Riding Hood, surprised and shaken, but safe and well.

The woodcutter dragged the wolf outside and threw him down a deep, dark well so he would never trouble anyone ever again. Then he, Granny and Little Red Riding Hood sat down to tea and ate all of the yummy goodies from Little Red Riding Hood's basket.

After tea, Little Red Riding Hood waved goodbye to her Granny and the woodcutter and ran all the way home to her mother, without straying once from the path or talking to any strangers. What an eventful day!